Little Women

Little Women

Abridged from the original by
Louisa May Alcott

Illustrations by
Ashley Mims

Published by Sourcebooks Jabberwocky, an imprint of Sourcebooks, Inc.
P.O. Box 4410, Naperville, Illinois 60567-4410
(630) 961-3900
Fax: (630) 961-2168
www.sourcebooks.com

Library of Congress Cataloging-in-Publication Data

Alcott, Louisa May, 1832-1888.
Little women : abridged from the original / by Louisa May Alcott.
p. cm.
Summary: An abridged version of the classic story that chronicles the joys and sorrows of the four March sisters as they grow into young women in mid-nineteenth-century New England.
ISBN-13: 978-1-4022-1169-0
ISBN-10: 1-4022-1169-4
[1. Sisters—Fiction. 2. Family life—New England—Fiction. 3. New England—History—19th century—Fiction.] I. Title.
PZ7.A335Li 2008
[Fic]--dc22

2008009127

Printed and bound in the United States of America.
LBM 10 9 8 7 6 5 4 3 2

Contents

PLAYING PILGRIMS

"Christmas won't be Christmas without any presents," grumbled Jo, lying on the rug.

"It's so dreadful to be poor!" sighed Meg, looking down at her old dress.

"I don't think it's fair for some girls to have plenty of pretty things, and other girls nothing at all," added little Amy.

"We've got Father and Mother, and each other," said Beth contentedly from her corner.

Jo said sadly, "We haven't got Father," thinking of Father far away, where the fighting was.

Margaret, was sixteen, and very pretty. Fifteen-year-old Jo was very tall, thin, and brown; her long, thick hair was her one beauty. Elizabeth, or Beth, as everyone called her, was a rosy, smooth haired, bright-eyed girl of thirteen, with a shy manner and a peaceful expression which was seldom disturbed. Amy, though the youngest, was a most important person, in her own opinion at least.

The clock struck six; Beth put a pair of slippers down to warm. Jo forgot how tired she was as she sat up to hold the slippers nearer to the blaze.

"They are quite worn out. Marmee must have a new pair."

"I'll tell you what we'll do," said Beth, "Let's each get her something for Christmas, and not get anything for ourselves."

"We must go shopping tomorrow afternoon, Meg," said Jo. "There is so much to do about the play for Christmas. In fact, we ought to rehearse tonight. Come here, Amy, and do the fainting scene, for you are as stiff as a poker in that."

"I don't see how you can write and act such splendid things, Jo. You're a regular Shakespeare!" exclaimed Beth.

"Not quite," replied Jo modestly. "But I'd like to try Macbeth; is that a dagger I see before me?" muttered Jo, rolling her eyes and clutching at the air, as she had seen a famous tragedian do.

"No, it's the toasting fork, with Mother's shoe on it instead of the bread," cried Meg, and the rehearsal ended in a general burst of laughter.

"Glad to find you so merry, my girls," said a cheery voice at the door, and actors and audience turned to welcome a tall, motherly lady.

Mrs. March got her wet things off, her warm slippers on, and sitting down in the easy chair, drew Amy to her lap, preparing to enjoy the happiest hour of her busy day. Mrs. March said, "I've got a treat for you after supper."

A quick, bright smile went round like a streak of sunshine.

"A letter! A letter! Three cheers for Father!"

"Yes, a nice long letter."

"Hurry and get done," cried Jo, choking on her tea and dropping her bread, butter side down, on the carpet in her haste to get at the treat.

"I think it was so splendid in Father to go as chaplain when he was too old to be drafted, and not strong enough for a soldier," said Meg warmly.

"When will he come home, Marmee?" asked Beth.

"Not for many months, dear, unless he is sick. Now come and hear the letter."

"...Give them all my dear love and a kiss. Tell them I think of them by day, pray for them by night, and find my best comfort in their affection at all times. I know they will remember all I said to them, that they will be loving children to you, and will do their duty faithfully, so that when I come back to them I may be fonder and prouder than ever of my little women."

Mrs. March broke the silence that followed by saying in her cheery voice, "Do you remember how you used to play Pilgrims Progress when you were little things? Now my little pilgrims, suppose you begin again, not in play, but in earnest, and see how far on you can get before Father comes home. Look under your pillows, Christmas morning, and you will find your guidebook."

A MERRY CHRISTMAS

Jo was the first to wake in the gray dawn of Christmas morning. No stockings hung at the fireplace. Then she remembered her mother's promise and, slipping her hand under her pillow, drew out a little crimson-covered book. She woke Meg with a "Merry Christmas," and bade her see what was under her pillow. A green-covered book appeared. Presently Beth and Amy woke to rummage and find their little books also, one dove-colored, the other blue.

"Where is Mother?" asked Meg, as she and Jo ran down to thank her for their gifts half an hour later.

"Goodness only knows. Some poor creeter came a-beggin', and your ma went straight off to see what was needed," replied Hannah, who had lived with the family since Meg was born, and was considered by them all more as a friend than a servant.

"She will be back soon, I think," said Meg, looking over the presents which were collected in a basket.

"There's Mother. Hide the basket, quick!" cried Jo, as a door slammed and steps sounded in the hall.

"Merry Christmas, Marmee! Thank you for our books," they all cried in chorus.

"Merry Christmas, little daughters! But I want to say one word before we sit down. Not far away from here lies a poor woman with a little newborn baby. Six children are huddled into one bed to keep from freezing, for they have no fire. There is nothing to eat over there, and the oldest boy came to tell me they were suffering hunger and cold. My girls, will you give them your breakfast as a Christmas present?"

They were all unusually hungry, having waited nearly an hour, and for a minute no one spoke; only a minute, for Jo exclaimed impetuously, "I'm so glad you came before we began!"

"I thought you'd do it," said Mrs. March, smiling as if satisfied. "You shall all go and help me, and when we come back we will have bread and milk for breakfast, and make it up at dinnertime."

They were soon ready, and the procession set out.

A poor, bare, miserable room it was, with broken windows, no fire, a sick mother, wailing baby, and a group of pale, hungry children cuddled under one old quilt, trying to keep warm.

How the big eyes stared and the blue lips smiled as the girls went in. Hannah, who had carried wood, made a fire. Mrs. March gave the mother tea and gruel, and comforted her with promises of help while she dressed the little baby as tenderly as if it had been her own. The girls meantime spread the table, set the children round

the fire, and fed them like so many hungry birds. That was a very happy breakfast, though they didn't get any of it. And when they went away, I think there were not in all the city four merrier people than the hungry little girls who gave away their breakfasts and contented themselves with bread and milk on Christmas morning.

"That's loving our neighbor better than ourselves," said Meg, as they set out their presents while their mother was upstairs collecting clothes for the poor Hummels.

"She's coming!" cried Jo.

Amy threw open the door, and Meg enacted escort with great dignity. Mrs. March was both surprised and touched, and smiled with her eyes full as she examined her presents and read the little notes which accompanied them.

The morning charities and ceremonies took so much time that the rest of the day was devoted to preparations for the evening festivities. No gentlemen were admitted, so Jo played male parts to her heart's content. The smallness of the company made it necessary for the two principal actors to take several parts apiece.

On Christmas night, a dozen girls piled onto the bed which was the dress circle, and sat before the blue and yellow chintz curtains in a most flattering state of expectancy. Presently a bell sounded, the curtains flew apart, and the operatic tragedy began.

Tumultuous applause followed its conclusion, but received an unexpected check, for the cot bed, on which the dress circle was built, suddenly shut up and extinguished the enthusiastic audience. The excitement had hardly subsided when Hannah appeared, with "Mrs. March's compliments, and would the ladies walk down to supper."

This was a surprise even to the actors, and when they saw the table, they looked at one another in rapturous amazement.

"Aunt March had a good fit and sent the supper," cried Jo with a sudden inspiration.

"Old Mr. Laurence sent it," replied Mrs. March.

"The Laurence boy's grandfather! What in the world put such a thing into his head? We don't know him!" exclaimed Meg.

"Hannah told one of his servants about your breakfast party. He is an odd old gentleman, but that pleased him. He knew my father years ago, and he sent me a polite note this afternoon, saying he hoped I would allow him to express his friendly feeling toward my children by sending them a few trifles in honor of the day."

"That boy put it into his head, I know he did! He's a capital fellow and I wish we could get acquainted," said Jo.

"I like his manners, so I've no objection to your knowing him, if a proper opportunity comes."

Chapter 3

The Laurence Boy

"Jo! Jo! Where are you?" cried Meg at the foot of the garret stairs.

"Here," answered a husky voice from above.

"Only see! A regular note of invitation from Mrs. Gardiner for tomorrow night," cried Meg.

"Mrs. Gardiner would be happy to see Miss March and Miss Josephine at a little dance on New Year's Eve. Marmee is willing we should go; now what shall we wear?"

"What's the use of asking that, when you know we shall wear our poplins, because we haven't got anything else?" answered Jo.

"If I only had a silk!" sighed Meg.

"I'm sure our pops look like silk, and they are nice enough for us. Yours is as good as new, but I forgot the burn and the tear in mine."

"You must sit still all you can and keep your back out of sight. The front is all right."

On New Year's Eve the parlor was deserted for the two younger girls played dressing maids and the two elder were absorbed in the all-important business of "getting ready for the party." There was a great deal of running up and down, laughing and talking, and at one time a strong smell of burned hair pervaded the house.

"Have a good time, dearies!" said Mrs. March, as the sisters went daintily down the walk.

"Now don't forget to keep the burnt patch out of sight, Jo. Is my sash right?" said Meg, as she turned from the glass in Mrs. Gardiner's dressing room after a prolonged prink.

"I know I shall forget. If you see me doing anything wrong, just remind me by a wink, will you?" returned Jo.

"No, winking isn't ladylike. I'll lift my eyebrows if anything is wrong, and nod if you are all right."

Down they went, feeling a trifle timid, for they seldom went to parties. Mrs. Gardiner greeted them kindly and handed them over to the eldest of her six daughters. Meg knew Sallie and was at her ease very soon; but Jo, who didn't care much for girls or girlish gossip, stood about, with her back carefully against the wall, and felt as much out of place as a colt in a flower garden. Jo saw a big red-headed youth approaching her corner, and fearing he meant to engage her she slipped into a curtained recess, intending to peep and enjoy herself in peace. Unfortunately, another bashful person had chosen the same refuge, for, as the curtain fell behind her, she found herself face to face with the "Laurence boy."

"I didn't know anyone was here!" stammered Jo, preparing to back out as speedily as she had bounced in.

But the boy laughed and said pleasantly, "Don't mind me, stay if you like."

Jo said, "You live near us, don't you?"

"Next door, Miss March."

"I am not Miss March, I'm only Jo," returned the young lady.

"I'm not Mr. Laurence, I'm only Laurie."

"Laurie Laurence, what an odd name."

"My first name is Theodore, but I don't like it."

"I hate my name too; I wish everyone would say Jo instead of Josephine. Don't you dance?"

"Sometimes. You see I've been abroad a good many years, and haven't been into company enough yet to know how you do things here."

"Abroad!" cried Jo. "Oh, tell me about it!"

Laurie didn't seem to know where to begin, but Jo's eager questions soon set him going.

Laurie was in the midst of an account of a students' festival at Heidelberg when Meg appeared in search of her sister. She beckoned, and Jo reluctantly followed her into a side room.

"I've sprained my ankle. It aches so, I can hardly stand, and I don't know how I'm ever going to get home," she said.

"I knew you'd hurt your feet with those silly shoes. I'm sorry. But I don't see what you can do, except get a carriage, or stay here all night," answered Jo, softly rubbing the poor ankle as she spoke.

"I can't have a carriage without its costing ever so much."

Jo was at her wits' end till she decided to take things into her own hands. She ran down and, finding a servant, asked if he could get her a carriage. It happened to be a hired waiter who knew nothing about the neighborhood and Jo was looking round for help when Laurie, who had heard what she said, came up and offered his grandfather's carriage, which had just come for him, he said.

"Please let me take you home. It's all on my way, you know, and it rains, they say."

That settled it, and telling him of Meg's mishap, Jo gratefully accepted and they rolled away in the luxurious close carriage, feeling very festive and elegant. Laurie went on the box so Meg could keep her foot up, and the girls talked over their party in freedom.

With many thanks, they said good night and crept in, hoping to disturb no one, but the instant their door creaked, two sleepy but eager voices cried out,

"Tell about the party! Tell about the party!"

Jo had saved some bonbons for the little girls, and they soon subsided, after hearing the most thrilling events of the evening.

Chapter 4

BURDENS

When Mr. March lost his property in trying to help an unfortunate friend, the two oldest girls begged to be allowed to do something toward their own support at least. Believing that they could not begin too early to cultivate energy, industry, and independence, their parents consented.

Margaret found a place as nursery governess and felt rich with her small salary.

Jo happened to suit Aunt March, who was lame and needed an active person to wait upon her. She had accepted the place since nothing better had appeared and, to everyone's surprise, got on remarkably well with her irascible relative. The real attraction was a large library of fine books, which was left to dust and spiders since Uncle March died. The dim, dusty room, the cozy chairs, and best of all, the wilderness of books in which she could wander where she liked, made the library a region of bliss to her.

The moment Aunt March took her nap, Jo hurried to this quiet place, and curling herself up in the easy chair, devoured poetry, romance, history, travels, and pictures like a regular bookworm.

Jo's ambition was to do something very splendid. What it was, she had no idea as yet, but left it for time to tell her. A quick temper, sharp tongue, and restless spirit were always getting her into scrapes.

Beth was too bashful to go to school, and she did her lessons at home with her father. Even when he went away, Beth went faithfully on by herself and did the best she could. She was a housewifely little creature and helped Hannah keep home neat and comfortable for the workers, never thinking of any reward but to be loved.

Beth had her troubles as well as the others, and not being an angel but a very human little girl, she often "wept a little weep" as Jo said, because she couldn't take music lessons and have a fine piano.

If anybody had asked Amy what the greatest trial of her life was, she would have answered at once, "My nose." When she was a baby, Jo had accidentally dropped her into the coal hod, and Amy insisted that the fall had ruined her nose forever.

Amy was in a fair way to be spoiled, for everyone petted her, and her small vanities and selfishnesses were growing nicely. One thing, however, rather quenched the vanities: she had to wear her cousin's clothes.

"My only comfort," she said to Meg, "is that Mother doesn't take tucks in my dresses whenever I'm naughty, as Maria Parks's mother does. It's really dreadful, for sometimes she is so bad her frock is up to her knees, and she can't come to school."

"Has anybody got anything to tell? It's been such a dismal day, I'm really dying for some amusement," said Meg.

"I saw something I liked this morning, and I meant to tell it at dinner, but I forgot," said Beth. "When I went to get some oysters for Hannah, Mr. Laurence was in the fish shop; but he didn't see me, for I kept behind the fish barrel, and he was busy with Mr. Cutter the fishman. A poor woman came in with a pail and a mop, and asked Mr. Cutter if he would let her do some scrubbing for a bit of fish, because she hadn't any dinner for her children. Mr. Cutter was in a hurry and said, "No," rather crossly. So she was going away, looking hungry and sorry, when Mr. Laurence hooked up a big fish with the crooked end of his cane and held it out to her. She was so glad and surprised, she took it right into her arms, and thanked him over and over. He told her to "go along and cook it," and she hurried off, so happy! Wasn't it good of him? Oh, she did look so funny, hugging the big, slippery fish, and hoping Mr. Laurence's bed in heaven would be 'aisy'."

Chapter 5

BEING NEIGHBORLY

"What in the world are you going to do now, Jo?" asked Meg one snowy afternoon, as her sister came tramping through the hall in rubber boots, old sack and hood, with a broom in one hand and a shovel in the other.

"Going out for exercise," answered Jo with a mischievous twinkle in her eyes.

She began to dig paths with great energy. The snow was light, and with her broom she soon swept a path all round the garden. Now the garden separated the Marches' house from that of Mr. Laurence. It was a stately stone mansion, and few people went in and out, except the old gentleman and his grandson.

"That boy is suffering for society and fun," she said to herself. "His grandpa does not know what's good for him, and keeps him shut up all alone. I've a great mind to go over and tell the old gentleman so!" Jo resolved to try what could be done. She saw Mr. Lawrence drive off, and then she paused and took a survey. All quiet, and nothing human visible but a curly black head leaning on a thin hand at the upper window.

"There he is," thought Jo. "Poor boy! It's a shame! I'll toss up a snowball and make him look out, and then say a kind word to him."

Up went a handful of soft snow, and the head turned at once, showing a face which lost its listless look in a minute, as the big eyes brightened and the mouth began to smile.

"How do you do?"

Laurie opened the window, and croaked out as hoarsely as a raven,

"I've had a bad cold, and been shut up a week."

"I'm sorry. What do you amuse yourself with?"

"Nothing."

"Don't you read?"

"Not much. They won't let me."

"Can't somebody read to you?"

"Grandpa does sometimes, but my books don't interest him, and I hate to ask my tutor, Mr. Brooke, all the time."

"Isn't there some nice girl who'd read and amuse you? Girls are quiet and like to play nurse. I'm not quiet and nice but I'll come, if Mother will let me. I'll go ask her. Shut the window like a good boy, and wait till I come."

Presently there came a loud ring, than a decided voice, asking for "Mr. Laurie," and a surprised-looking servant came running up to announce a young lady.

"Here I am. Mother sent her love, and was glad if I could do anything for you. Meg wanted me to bring some of her blancmange, and Beth thought her cats would be comforting. Shall I read aloud?" And Jo looked affectionately toward some inviting books near by.

"Thank you! I've read all those, and if you don't mind, I'd rather talk," answered Laurie.

"Not a bit. I'll talk all day if you'll only set me going. Beth says I never know when to stop."

"Is Beth the rosy one, who stays at home a good deal and sometimes goes out with a little basket?" asked Laurie with interest.

"Yes, that's Beth."

"The pretty one is Meg, and the curly-haired one is Amy, I believe?"

"How did you find that out?"

"Why, you see I often hear you calling to one another. I beg your pardon for being so rude, but sometimes you forget to pull down the curtain at the window where the flowers are. And when the lamps are lighted, it's like looking at a picture to see the fire, and you all around the table with your mother."

The solitary, hungry look in his eyes went straight to Jo's warm heart.

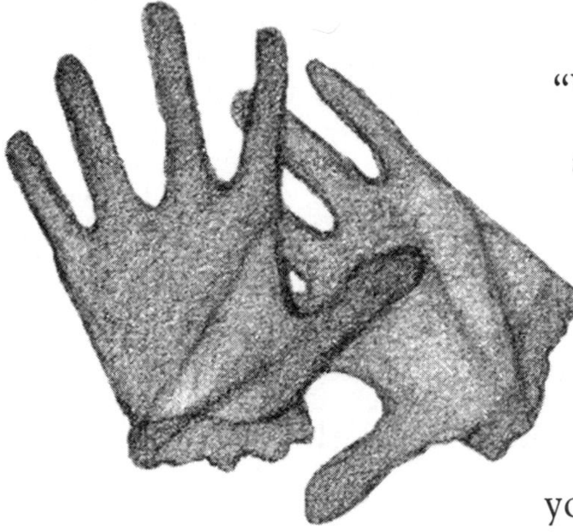

"We'll never draw that curtain anymore, and I give you leave to look as much as you like. I just wish, though, you'd come over and see us. Wouldn't your grandpa let you?"

"I think he would, if your mother asked him."

"We want to know you. We haven't been here a great while, you know, but we have got acquainted with all our neighbors but you."

"Mr. Brooke, my tutor, doesn't stay here, you know, and I have no one to go about with me, so I just stop at home and get on as I can."

Then they got to talking about books, and to Jo's delight, she found that Laurie loved them as well as she did, and had read even more than herself.

"If you like them so much, come down and see ours," said Laurie, getting up.

"What richness!" sighed Jo, gazing about her with an air of intense satisfaction. "Theodore Laurence, you ought to be the happiest boy in the world."

"A fellow can't live on books," said Laurie.

Before he could say more, a bell rang, and Jo flew up, exclaiming with alarm, "Mercy me! It's your grandpa!"

"The doctor to see you, sir," and the maid beckoned as she spoke.

Laurie went away, and his guest amused herself in her own way.

Chapter 6

THE GRAND PIANO

She was standing before a fine portrait of the old gentleman when the door opened again, and without turning, she said decidedly, "I'm sure now that I shouldn't be afraid of him, for he's got kind eyes, though his mouth is grim, and he looks as if he had a tremendous will of his own. He isn't as handsome as my grandfather, but I like him."

"Thank you, ma'am," said a gruff voice behind her, and there, to her great dismay, stood old Mr. Laurence.

Poor Jo blushed till she couldn't blush any redder, and her heart began to beat uncomfortably fast as she thought what she had said.

"So you're not afraid of me, hey?"

"Not much, sir."

"And you don't think me as handsome as your grandfather?"

"Not quite, sir."

"And I've got a tremendous will, have I?"

"I only said I thought so."

"But you like me in spite of it?"

"Yes, I do, sir."

That answer pleased the old gentleman. "You've got your grandfather's spirit. He was a fine man, my dear, but what is better, he was a brave and an honest one, and I was proud to be his friend."

"Thank you, sir," and Jo was quite comfortable after that.

"There's the tea bell. Come down and go on being neighborly."

The old gentleman did not say much as he drank his four cups of tea, but he watched the young people, who soon chatted away like old friends, and the change in his grandson did not escape him. There was color, light, and life in the boy's face now.

Jo's attention was then taken by a grand piano, which stood open.

"Do you play?" she asked, turning to Laurie with a respectful expression.

"Sometimes," he answered modestly.

"Please do now. I want to hear it, so I can tell Beth."

So Laurie played and Jo listened. Her respect and regard for the "Laurence boy" increased very much, for he played remarkably well and didn't put on any airs. She wished Beth could hear him, but she did not say so, only praised him till he was quite abashed and his grandfather came to his rescue.

"That will do, that will do young lady. Too many sugarplums are not good for him. His music isn't bad, but I hope he will do as well in more important things. Going? Well I'm much obliged to you and I hope you'll come again. My respects to your mother. Good night, Doctor Jo."

He shook hands kindly, but looked as if something did not please him. When they got into the hall, Jo asked Laurie if she had said something amiss.

"No, it was me. He doesn't like to hear me play."

"Why not?"

"I'll tell you some day—you will come again, I hope?"

"If you promise to come and see us after you are well."

"I will."

"Good night, Laurie!"

"Good night, Jo."

"Mother, why didn't Mr. Laurence like to have Laurie play?" asked Jo.

"I think it was because his son, Laurie's father, married an Italian lady, a musician, which displeased the old man who was very proud. The lady was good and lovely and accomplished, but he did not like her, and never saw his son after he married. They both died when Laurie was a little child, and then his grandfather took him home. I fancy the boy, who was born in Italy, is not very strong, and the old man is afraid of losing him, which makes him so careful. Laurie comes naturally by his love of music, and I dare say his grandfather fears that he may want to be a musician."

"How silly!" said Jo. "Let him be a musician if he wants to, and not plague his life out sending him to college, when he hates to go... We'll all be good to him because he hasn't got any mother—and he may come over and see us, mayn't he, Marmee?"

"Yes, Jo, your little friend is very welcome."

Chapter 7

BETH FINDS THE PALACE BEAUTIFUL

Everyone liked Laurie, and he privately informed his tutor that "the Marches were regularly splendid girls."

What good times they had, to be sure! Meg could walk in the conservatory whenever she liked. Jo browsed over the new library voraciously, and convulsed the old gentleman with her criticisms. Amy copied pictures and enjoyed beauty to her heart's content, and Laurie played "Lord of the manor" in the most delightful style. But Beth, though yearning for the grand piano, could not pluck up courage to go to the "Mansion of Bliss," as Meg called it. No persuasions or enticements could overcome her fear, till, the fact coming to Mr. Laurence's ear in some mysterious way, he set about mending matters. During one of the brief calls he made, he artfully led the conversation to music, and told such charming anecdotes that Beth found it impossible to stay in her distant corner, but crept nearer and nearer. Mr. Laurence talked on about Laurie's lessons and teachers. And presently, as if the idea had just occurred to him, he said to Mrs. March,

"The boy neglects his music now, and I'm glad of it, for he was getting too fond of it. But the piano suffers for want of use. Wouldn't some of your girls like to run over and practice on it now and then? They needn't see or speak to anyone, but run in at any time. For I'm shut up in my study at the other end of the house, and the servants are never near the drawing room after nine o'clock."

Here he rose, as if going, and as a little hand slipped into his, Beth looked up at him with a face full of gratitude.

"Are you the musical girl?" he asked as he looked down at her very kindly.

"I'm Beth. I love it dearly, and I'll come, if you are quite sure nobody will hear me, and be disturbed."

"Not a soul, my dear, and I shall be obliged to you."

"How kind you are, sir!"

The old gentleman softly stroked the hair off her forehead, "I had a little girl once, with eyes like these. God bless you, my dear!"

Next day, having seen both the old and young gentlemen out of the house, Beth fairly got in at the side door, and made her way as noiselessly as any mouse to the drawing room; and with trembling fingers and frequent stops to listen and look about, Beth at last touched the great instrument, and straightway forgot her fear, herself, and everything else but the unspeakable delight which the music gave her, for it was like the voice of a beloved friend.

After that the little brown hood slipped through the hedge nearly every day, and the great drawing room was haunted by a tuneful spirit that came and went unseen.

"Mother, I'm going to work Mr. Laurence a pair of slippers. He is so kind to me, I must thank him, and I don't know any other way. Can I do it?" asked Beth.

"Yes, dear. It will please him very much."

Beth worked away early and late, and the slippers were finished before anyone got tired of them. Then she wrote a short, simple note, and with Laurie's help, got them smuggled onto the study table one morning before the old gentleman was up. Beth waited to see what would happen.

On the afternoon of the second day, she went out to do an errand. As she came up the street, on her return, several joyful voices screamed,

"Here's a letter from the old gentleman! Come quick, and read it!"

At the door her sisters seized and bore her to the parlor in a triumphal procession, all pointing and all saying at once, "Look there! Look there!" Beth did look, and turned pale with delight and surprise, for there stood a little cabinet piano, with a letter lying on the glossy lid directed like a sign board to "Miss Elizabeth March."

"For me?" gasped Beth, holding onto Jo. "You read it! I can't, I feel so queer!"

"Miss March: Dear Madam—I have had many pairs of slippers in my life, but I never had any that suited me so well as yours. These will always remind me of the gentle giver. I like to pay my debts, so I know you will allow 'the old gentleman' to send you something which once belonged to the little granddaughter he lost. With hearty thanks and best wishes, I remain 'your grateful friend and humble servant, JAMES LAURENCE.'"

“Try it, honey,” said Hannah, who always took a share in the family joys and sorrows.

So Beth tried it, and everyone pronounced it the most remarkable piano ever heard.

TRACK 8

Chapter 8

SECRETS

Jo was very busy in the garret, for the October days began to grow chilly, and the afternoons were short. For two or three hours the sun lay warmly in thc high window, showing Jo seated on the old sofa, writing busily, with her papers spread out upon a trunk before her. Quite absorbed in her work, Jo scribbled away till the last page was filled, when she signed her name with a flourish and threw down her pen, exclaiming,

"There, I've done my best!"

Jo picked up another manuscript, and, putting both in her pocket, crept quietly downstairs. She went off at a great pace till she reached a certain number in a certain busy street. She went into the doorway, looked up the dirty stairs, and after standing stock still a minute, suddenly dived into the street and walked away as rapidly as she came. This maneuver she repeated several times, to the great amusement of a black-eyed young gentleman lounging in the window of a building opposite. On returning for the third time, Jo gave herself a shake, and walked up the stairs, looking as if she were going to have all her teeth out.

There was a dentist's sign, among others which adorned the entrance, and after staring a moment at the pair of artificial jaws which slowly opened and shut to draw attention to a fine set of teeth, the young gentleman put on his coat, took his hat, and went down to post himself in the opposite doorway. In ten minutes, Jo came running downstairs with a very red face and the general appearance of a person who had just passed through a trying ordeal of some sort. When she saw the young gentleman, she looked anything but pleased, and passed him with a nod. But he followed, asking with an air of sympathy, "Did you have a bad time?"

"Not very."

"Why did you go alone?"

"Didn't want anyone to know."

"How many did you have out?"

Jo looked at her friend as if she did not understand him, then began to laugh as if mightily amused at something.

"What are you laughing at? You are up to some mischief, Jo," said Laurie, looking mystified.

"So are you. What were you doing, sir, up in that billiard saloon?"

"It wasn't a billiard saloon, but a gymnasium, and I was taking a lesson in fencing."

Laurie walked in silence a few minutes.

"I'd like to walk with you and tell you something very interesting. It's a secret, and if I tell you, you must tell me yours."

"I haven't got any," began Jo, but stopped suddenly, remembering that she had. "You'll not say anything about it at home, will you?"

"Not a word."

"Well, I've left two stories with a newspaperman, and he's to give his answer next week," whispered Jo in her confidant's ear. "It won't come to anything, I dare say, but I couldn't rest till I had tried."

"Why, Jo, your stories are works of Shakespeare compared to half the rubbish that is published every day. Won't it be fun to see them in print, and shan't we feel proud of our authoress?"

"Where's your secret?"

"I may get into a scrape for telling, but I didn't promise not to. I know where Meg's glove is."

"Is that all?" said Jo, looking disappointed.

"It's quite enough for the present, as you'll agree when I tell you where it is."

Laurie bent, and whispered three words in Jo's ear.

She stood and stared at him for a minute, looking both surprised and displeased, then walked on, saying sharply, "How do you know?"

"Saw it."

"Where?"

"Pocket."

"It's ridiculous, it won't be allowed. What would Meg say?"

"You are not to tell anyone."

"I didn't promise."

"That was understood, and I trusted you."

"Well, I won't for the present, anyway, but I'm disgusted, and wish you hadn't told me."

"I thought you'd be pleased."

"At the idea of anybody coming to take Meg away? No, thank you."

For a week or two, Jo behaved so queerly that her sisters were quite bewildered. She rushed to the door when the postman rang, was rude to Mr. Brooke whenever they met, would sit looking at Meg with a woe-begone face, occasionally jumping up to shake and then kiss her in a very mysterious manner. On the second Saturday, Meg was scandalized by the sight of Laurie chasing Jo all over the garden and finally capturing her in Amy's bower. Shrieks of laughter were heard, followed by the murmur of voices and a great flapping of newspapers. In a few minutes Jo bounced in, laid herself on the sofa, and affected to read.

"Have you anything interesting there?" asked Meg, with condescension.

"Nothing but a story, won't amount to much, I guess," returned Jo.

"You'd better read it aloud. That will amuse us and keep you out of mischief," said Amy in her most grown-up tone.

"What's the name?" asked Beth.

"The Rival Painters."

"That sounds well. Read it," said Meg.

With a loud "Hem!" and a long breath, Jo began to read very fast. The girls listened with interest, for the tale was romantic, and somewhat pathetic, as most of the characters died in the end.

"Who wrote it?" asked Beth.

The reader suddenly sat up and replied in a loud voice, "Your sister."

"You?" cried Meg.

"It's very good," said Amy critically.

"I knew it! I knew it! Oh, my Jo, I am so proud!" And Beth ran to hug her sister and exult over this splendid success.

Having told how she disposed of her tales, Jo added, "And when I went to get my answer, the man said he liked them both, but didn't pay beginners, only let them print in his paper. It was good practice, he said, and when the beginners improved, anyone would pay. So I let him have the two stories, and today this was sent to me, and Laurie caught me with it and insisted on seeing it, so I let him. And he said it was good, and I shall write more, and he's going to get the next paid for."

Chapter 9

A Telegram

"November is the most disagreeable month in the whole year," said Margaret, standing at the window one dull afternoon, looking out at the frostbitten garden.

"If something very pleasant should happen now, we should think it a delightful month," said Beth.

Jo groaned, but Beth, who sat at the other window, said smiling, "Two pleasant things are going to happen right away. Marmee is coming down the street, and Laurie is tramping through the garden as if he had something nice to tell."

In they both came, Mrs. March with her usual question, "Any letter from Father, girls?" and Laurie to say in his persuasive way, "Won't some of you come for a drive? I've been working away at mathematics till my head is in a muddle and I'm going to take Brooke home. Come, Jo, you and Beth will go, won't you?"

"Of course we will."

"Much obliged, but I'm busy." And Meg whisked out her workbasket.

"Can I do anything for you, Madam Mother?" asked Laurie.

"No, thank you—"

A sharp ring interrupted her, and a minute after, Hannah came in with a letter.

"It's one of them horrid telegraph things, mum," she said, handling it as if she was afraid it would explode and do some damage. Mrs. March snatched it, read the two lines it contained, and dropped back into her chair as white as if the little paper had sent a bullet to her heart.

Jo read aloud, in a frightened voice,

"Mrs. March: Your husband is very ill. Come at once. S. HALE, Blank Hospital, Washington."

Mrs. March was herself again directly, read the message over, and stretched out her arms to her daughters, saying, "I shall go at once, but it may be too late. Oh, children, children, help me to bear it!"

"Where's Laurie?" she asked presently, when she had collected her thoughts and decided on the first duties to be done.

"Here, ma'am," cried the boy.

"Send a telegram saying I will come at once. The next train goes early in the morning. I'll take that."

"What else? The horses are ready. I can go anywhere, do anything."

"Leave a note at Aunt March's. Jo, give me that pen and paper."

Jo drew the table before her mother, well knowing that money for the long, sad journey must be borrowed.

"Jo, get these things. They'll be needed and I must go prepared for nursing. Hospital stores are not always good. Beth, go and ask Mr. Laurence for a couple of bottles of old wine. I'm not too proud to beg for Father. He shall have the best of everything."

Mr. Laurence came hurrying back with Beth, bringing every comfort the kind old gentleman could think of for the invalid, and friendliest promises of protection for the girls during the mother's absence, which comforted her very much. Then Meg ran through the entry, and came suddenly upon Mr. Brooke.

"I'm very sorry to hear of this, Miss March," he said, in the kind, quiet tone which sounded very pleasantly to her perturbed spirit. "I came to offer myself as escort to your mother. Mr. Laurence has commissions for me in Washington, and it will give me real satisfaction to be of service to her there."

Meg put out her hand, with a face so full of gratitude that Mr. Brooke would have felt repaid for a much greater sacrifice than the trifling one of time and comfort which he was about to take.

"How kind you all are! Thank you very, very much!"

Everything was arranged by the time Laurie returned with a note from Aunt March, enclosing the desired sum, and a few lines repeating what she had often said before, that she had always told them it was absurd for March to go into the army, and she hoped they would take her advice the next time.

The short afternoon wore away, but still Jo did not come. They began to get anxious, and Laurie went off to find her, for no one knew what freak Jo might take into her head. He missed her, however, and she came walking in with a very queer expression of countenance, which puzzled the family as much as did the roll of bills she laid before her mother, saying with a little choke in her voice, "That's my contribution toward making Father comfortable and bringing him home!"

"Twenty-five dollars! Jo, I hope you haven't done anything rash!"

"No, it's mine honestly for I only sold what was my own."

As she spoke, Jo took off her bonnet, and a general outcry arose, for all her abundant hair was cut short.

"Your hair! Your beautiful hair! Oh, Jo, how could you? Your one beauty."

"She doesn't look like my Jo any more, but I love her dearly for it!"

As everyone exclaimed, and Beth hugged the cropped head tenderly, Jo assumed an indifferent air, which did not deceive anyone a particle, "It will be good for my vanity; I was getting too proud of my wig. It will do my brains good to have that mop taken off. I'm satisfied, so please take the money and let's have supper."

No one wanted to go to bed when at ten o'clock Mrs. March put by the last finished job, and said, "Come girls. Go to bed and don't talk, for we must be up early and shall need all the sleep we can get. Good night, my darlings."

Chapter 10

LETTERS

In the cold gray dawn the sisters lit their lamp and read their chapter with an earnestness never felt before. For now the shadow of a real trouble had come, the little books were full of help and comfort, and as they dressed, they agreed to say good-bye cheerfully and hopefully, and send their mother on her anxious journey unsaddened by tears or complaints from them. Nobody talked much, but as the time drew very near and they sat waiting for the carriage, Mrs. March said to the girls,

"Children, I leave you to Hannah's care and Mr. Laurence's protection. Hope and keep busy, and whatever happens, remember that you never can be fatherless."

"Meg, dear, be prudent, watch over your sisters, consult Hannah, and in any perplexity, go to Mr. Laurence. Be patient, Jo; don't get despondent or do rash things, write to me often, and be my brave girl. Beth, comfort yourself with your music, and you Amy, help all you can, and keep happy safe at home."

The rattle of an approaching carriage made them all start and listen. Their hearts were very heavy as they sent loving messages to Father, remembering, as they spoke, that it might be too late to deliver them. They kissed their mother quietly, and tried to wave their hands cheerfully when she drove away.

Laurie and his grandfather came over to see her off, and Mr. Brooke looked so strong and sensible and kind that the girls christened him "Mr. Greatheart" on the spot.

"Good-bye, my darlings! God bless and keep us all!" whispered Mrs. March.

"Meg, I wish you'd go and see the Hummels. You know Mother told us not to forget them," said Beth, ten days after Mrs. March's departure.

"I'm too tired to go this afternoon," replied Meg. "Why don't you go yourself?"

"I have been every day, but the baby is sick, and I don't know what to do for it."

Beth spoke earnestly, and Meg promised she would go tomorrow.

An hour passed. Meg went to her room to try on a new dress, Jo was absorbed in her story, and Hannah was sound asleep before the kitchen fire, when Beth quietly put on her hood, filled her basket with odds and ends for the poor children, and went out into the chilly air. It was late when she came back, and no one saw her creep upstairs and shut herself into her mother's room. Half an hour after, Jo went to Mother's closet for something and there found little Beth sitting on the medicine chest, looking very grave, with red eyes and a camphor bottle in her hand.

"What's the matter?" cried Jo, as Beth put out her hand as if to warn her off.

"You've had the scarlet fever, haven't you?"

"Years ago, when Meg did. Why?"

"Oh, Jo, the baby's dead!"

"What baby?"

"Mrs. Hummel's. It died in my lap before she got home," cried Beth with a sob.

"My poor dear, how dreadful for you!" said Jo, taking her sister in her arms. "Don't cry, dear! What did you do?"

"I just sat and held it softly till Mrs. Hummel came with the doctor. He said it was dead, and looked at Heinrich and Minna, who have sore throats. 'Scarlet fever, ma'am. Ought to have called me before,' he said crossly. It was very sad, and I cried with them till he turned round all of a sudden and told me to go home and take belladonna right away, or I'd have the fever."

"If Mother was only at home!" exclaimed Jo.

"Now I'll tell you what we'll do," said Hannah, when she had examined and questioned Beth. "We will have Dr. Bangs, just to take a look at you, dear, and see that we start right. Then we'll send Amy off to Aunt March's for a spell, to keep her out of harm's way."

Amy rebelled outright, and passionately declared that she had rather have the fever than go to Aunt March. Laurie walked into the parlor to find Amy sobbing, with her head in the sofa cushions. She told her story, expecting to be consoled, but Laurie only put his hands in his pockets and walked about the room, whistling softly. Presently he sat down beside her, and said, "Don't cry, but hear what a jolly plan I've got. You go to Aunt March's, and I'll come and take you out every day. Won't that be better than moping here?"

"Well—I guess I will," said Amy slowly.

"Good girl!" said Laurie, with an approving pat.

Meg and Jo came running down to behold the miracle which had been wrought, and Amy, feeling very precious and self-sacrificing, promised to go, if the doctor said Beth was going to be ill.

"Tell me if I shall telegraph to your mother, or do anything?" asked Laurie.

"That is what troubles me," said Meg. "I think we ought to tell her if Beth is really ill, but Hannah says we mustn't, for Mother can't leave Father, and it will only make them anxious."

"Hum, well, I can't say. Suppose you ask Grandfather after the doctor has been."

"We will. Jo, go and get Dr. Bangs at once," commanded Meg.

Dr. Bangs came, said Beth had symptoms of the fever, but he thought she would have it lightly, though he looked sober over the Hummel story. Amy was ordered off at once, and provided with something to ward off danger.

DARK DAYS

Beth did have the fever, and was much sicker than anyone but Hannah and the doctor suspected. Meg stayed at home, and kept house, feeling very anxious and a little guilty when she wrote letters in which no mention was made of Beth's illness.

Jo devoted herself to Beth, day and night. Beth was very patient, but there came a time when during the fever fits she began to talk in a hoarse, broken voice, to play on the coverlet as if on her beloved little piano, and try to sing with a throat so swollen that there was no music left; a time when she did not know the familiar faces around her, and called imploringly for her mother. Then Jo grew frightened; Meg begged to be allowed to write the truth, and even Hannah said she would think of it, though there was no danger yet.

How dark the days seemed now, how sad and lonely the house, everyone missed Beth.

She lay hour after hour, tossing to and fro, with incoherent words on her lips, or sank into a heavy sleep which brought her no refreshment. Dr. Bangs came twice a day, Hannah sat up at night, Meg kept a telegram in her desk all ready to send off at any minute, and Jo never stirred from Beth's side.

The first of December was a wintry day indeed to them, for a bitter wind blew, snow fell fast, and the year seemed getting ready for its death. When Dr. Bangs came that morning, he looked long at Beth, held the hot hand in both his own for a minute, and laid it gently down, saying, in a low voice to Hannah, "If Mrs. March can leave her husband, she'd better be sent for."

Hannah nodded without speaking, for her lips twitched nervously; Meg dropped down into a chair as the strength seemed to go out of her limbs at the sound of those words; and Jo, standing with a pale face for a minute, ran to the parlor, snatched up the telegram, and throwing on her things, rushed out into the storm.

She was soon back, and, while noiselessly taking off her cloak, Laurie came in with a letter, saying that Mr. March was mending again. Jo read it thankfully, but the heavy weight did not seem lifted off her heart, and her face was so full of misery that Laurie asked quickly, "What is it? Is Beth worse?"

"I've sent for Mother," said Jo.

"Good for you, Jo! Did you do it on your own responsibility?" asked Laurie.

"No. The doctor told us to."

"Oh, Jo," cried Laurie, with a startled face.

As the tears streamed fast down poor Jo's cheeks, she stretched out her hand in a helpless sort of way, as if groping in the dark, and Laurie took it in his, whispering as well as he could with a lump in his throat, "I'm here. Hold on to me, Jo, dear!"

Soon she dried the tears which had relieved her.

"Thank you, Teddy, I'm better now. I don't feel so forlorn, and will try to bear it if it comes."

"Keep hoping for the best. Soon your mother will be here, and then everything will be all right."

"I'm so glad Father is better. Now she won't feel so bad about leaving him."

"Poor girl, you're worn out. Stop a bit. I'll hearten you up in a jiffy."

"I telegraphed to your mother yesterday, and Brooke answered she'd come at once, and she'll be here tonight, and everything will be all right. Aren't you glad I did it?"

Jo grew quite white, "Oh, Laurie! Oh, Mother! I am so glad! Tell me all about it."

"Why, you see I got fidgety, and so did Grandpa. We

thought Hannah was overdoing the authority business, and your mother ought to know. So I got Grandpa to say it was high time we did something, and off I pelted to the office yesterday. Your mother will come, I know, and the late train is in at 2 a.m."

"Bless you, Teddy. Bless you."

A breath of fresh air seemed to blow through the house. Everyone rejoiced but Beth. She lay in that heavy stupor, the once rosy face so changed and vacant, and the once pretty, well-kept hair scattered rough and tangled on the pillow. All day she lay so, and all day the snow fell, the bitter wind raged, and the hours dragged slowly by. But night came at last. The doctor had been in to say that some change, for better or worse, would probably take place about midnight.

Chapter 12

THE FEVER TURNS

The girls never forgot that night. It was past two, when Jo, who stood at the window thinking how dreary the world looked in its winding sheet of snow, heard a movement by the bed, and turning quickly, saw Meg kneeling before their mother's easy chair with her face hidden. A dreadful fear passed coldly over Jo, as she thought, "Beth is dead."

She was back at her post in an instant, and to her excited eyes a great change seemed to have taken place. The fever flush and the look of pain were gone, and the beloved little face looked so pale and peaceful in its utter repose that Jo felt no desire to weep or to lament. She kissed the damp forehead with her heart on her lips and softly whispered, "Good-bye, my Beth. Good-bye."

Hannah started out of her sleep, hurried to the bed, looked at Beth, felt her hands, listened at her lips, and then, sat down to rock to and fro, exclaiming under her breath, "The fever's turned! Praise be given!"

Before the girls could believe the happy truth, the doctor came to confirm it. "Yes, my dears, I think the little girl will pull through this time."

"If Mother would only come now!" said Jo, as the winter night began to wane.

Never had the sun risen so beautifully, and never had the world seemed so lovely as it did to the heavy eyes of Meg and Jo, as they looked out in the early morning, when their long, sad vigil was done.

"It looks like a fairy world," said Meg, smiling to herself.

"Hark!" cried Jo, starting to her feet.

Yes, there was a sound of bells at the door below, and then Laurie's voice saying in a joyful whisper, "Girls, she's come! She's come!"

That evening, while Meg was writing to her father to report the traveler's safe arrival, Jo slipped upstairs into Beth's room, and finding her mother in her usual place, stood a minute twisting her fingers in her hair, with a worried gesture and an undecided look.

"I want to tell you something, Mother. Last summer Meg left a pair of gloves over at the Laurences' and only one was returned. We forgot about it, till Teddy told me that Mr. Brooke owned that he liked Meg but didn't dare say so, she was so young and he so poor. Now, isn't that a dreadful state of things?"

"Then you fancy that Meg is not interested in John?"

"Who?" cried Jo, staring.

"Mr. Brooke. I call him 'John' now. We fell into the way of doing so at the hospital, and he likes it."

"Oh, dear! I know you'll take his part. He's been good to Father, and you won't send him away, but let Meg marry him, if she wants to."

"My dear, don't get angry about it, and I will tell you how it happened. John went with me at Mr. Laurence's request, and was so devoted to poor Father that we couldn't help getting fond of him. He was perfectly open and honorable about Meg, for he told us he loved her, but would earn a comfortable home before he asked her to marry him. He only wanted our leave to love her and work for her, and the right to make her love him if he could. He is a truly excellent young man, and we could not refuse to listen to him, but I will not consent to Meg's engaging herself so young. Jo, I confide in you and don't wish you to say anything to Meg yet. When John comes back, and I see them together, I can judge better of her feelings toward him."

Jo leaned her chin on her knees in a disconsolate attitude.

"Jo, it is natural and right you should all go to homes of your own in time, but I do want to keep my girls as long as I can, and I am sorry that this happened so soon, for Meg is only seventeen and it will be some years before John can make a home for her. Your father and I have agreed that she shall not bind herself in any way, nor be married, before twenty."

"Hadn't you rather have her marry a rich man?" asked Jo.

"I am content to see Meg begin humbly, for if I am not mistaken, she will be rich in the possession of a good man's heart, and that is better than a fortune."

Chapter 13

CONFIDENTIAL

The kiss her mother gave Jo was a very tender one, and as she went away, Mrs. March reflected, with a mixture of satisfaction and regret, "Meg may not love John yet, but will soon learn to."

Like sunshine after a storm were the peaceful weeks which followed. The invalids improved rapidly, and Mr. March began to talk of returning early in the new year. Beth was soon able to lie on the study sofa all day.

Several days of unusually mild weather fitly ushered in a splendid Christmas Day. Hannah "felt in her bones" that it

was going to be an unusually fine day, and she proved herself a true prophetess. To begin with, Mr. March wrote that he should soon be with them, then Beth felt uncommonly well that morning, and, being dressed in her mother's gift, a soft crimson merino wrapper, was borne in high triumph to the window to behold the offering of Jo and Laurie. Out in the garden stood a stately snow maiden, crowned with holly, bearing a basket of fruit and flowers in one hand, a great roll of music in the other, a perfect rainbow of an Afghan round her chilly shoulders, and a Christmas carol issuing from her lips on a pink paper streamer.

"I'm so full of happiness, that if Father was only here, I couldn't hold one drop more," said Beth, quite sighing with contentment.

Half an hour after everyone had said they were so happy they could only hold one drop more, the drop came. Laurie opened the parlor door and popped his head in very quietly.

"Here's another Christmas present for the March family."

Before the words were well out of his mouth, he was whisked away somehow, and in his place appeared a tall man, leaning on the arm of another tall man, who tried to say something and couldn't.

Mr. March became invisible in the embrace of four pairs of loving arms. Mr. Brooke kissed Meg entirely by mistake, as he somewhat incoherently explained. Mrs. March was the first to recover herself, "Hush! Remember Beth."

But it was too late. The study door flew open, the little red wrapper appeared on the threshold, joy put strength into the feeble limbs, and Beth ran straight into her father's arms.

Mr. March told how he had longed to surprise them, and how, when the fine weather came, he had been allowed by his doctor to take advantage of it, how devoted Brooke had been, and how he was altogether a most estimable and upright young man.

There never was such a Christmas dinner as they had that day. Mr. Laurence and his grandson dined with them, also Mr. Brooke, at whom Jo glowered darkly, to Laurie's infinite amusement. A sleigh ride had been planned, but the girls would not leave their father, so the guests departed early, and as twilight gathered, the happy family sat together round the fire.

"Just a year ago we were groaning over the dismal Christmas we expected to have. Do you remember?" asked Jo.

"Rather a pleasant year on the whole!" said Meg, smiling at the fire, and congratulating herself on having treated Mr. Brooke with dignity.

"I'm glad it's over, because we've got you back," whispered Beth, who sat on her father's knee.

Chapter 14

AUNT MARCH SETTLES THE QUESTION

Like bees swarming after their queen, mother and daughters hovered about Mr. March the next day, neglecting everything to look at, wait upon, and listen to the new invalid, who was in a fair way to be killed by kindness. Laurie went by in the afternoon, and seeing Meg at the window, seemed suddenly possessed with a melodramatic fit, for he fell down on one knee in the snow, beat his breast, tore his hair, and clasped his hands imploringly.

"What does the goose mean?" said Meg.

"He's showing you how your John will go on by-and-by. Touching, isn't it?" answered Jo scornfully.

"Don't say my John, it isn't proper or true," but Meg's voice lingered over the words as if they sounded pleasant to her. "Please don't plague me, Jo, I've told you I don't care much about him."

"I don't mean to plague you but I do wish it was all settled. I hate to wait, so if you mean ever to do it, make haste and have it over quickly," said Jo, pettishly.

"I can't say anything till he speaks, and he won't, because Father said I was too young," began Meg, bending over her work with a queer little smile.

"If he did speak, you wouldn't know what to say, but would cry or blush, instead of giving a good, decided 'No'."

"I'm not so silly and weak as you think. I know just what I should say, for I've planned it all, so I needn't be taken unawares."

"Would you mind telling me what you'd say?" asked Jo, more respectfully.

"Not at all. I should merely say, quite calmly and decidedly, 'Thank you, Mr. Brooke, you are very kind, but I agree with Father that I am too young to enter into any engagement at present, so please say no more, but let us be friends as we were.'"

"Hum, that's stiff and cool enough! I don't believe you'll ever say it, and I know he won't be satisfied if you do. If he goes on like the rejected lovers in books, you'll give in, rather than hurt his feelings."

"No, I won't. I shall tell him I've made up my mind, and shall walk out of the room with dignity."

Meg rose as she spoke, and was just going to rehearse the dignified exit, when a step in the hall made her fly into her seat and began to sew as fast as if her life depended on finishing that particular seam in a given time. Jo smothered a laugh at the sudden change and when someone gave a modest tap, opened the door with a grim aspect which was anything but hospitable.

"Good afternoon. I came to get my umbrella, that is, to see how your father finds himself today," said Mr. Brooke, getting a trifle confused as his eyes went from one telltale face to the other.

Jo slipped out of the room to give Meg a chance to make her speech. But the instant she vanished, Meg began to sidle toward the door, murmuring,

"Mother will like to see you. I'll call her."

"Don't go. Are you afraid of me, Margaret?" And Mr. Brooke looked so hurt that Meg thought she must have done something very rude. Anxious to appear friendly and at her ease, she put out her hand with a confiding gesture and said gratefully,

"How can I be afraid when you have been so kind to Father? I only wish I could thank you for it."

"Shall I tell you how?" asked Mr. Brooke, holding the small hand fast in both his own, and looking down at Meg with so much love in the brown eyes that her heart began to flutter, and she both longed to run away and to stop and listen.

"Oh no, please don't," she said.

"I won't trouble you. I only want to know if you care for me a little, Meg. I love you so much, dear," added Mr. Brooke tenderly.

This was the moment for the calm, proper speech, but Meg didn't make it. She forgot every word of it, hung her head, and answered, "I don't know."

"Will you try and find out? I want to know so much, for I can't go to work with any heart until I learn whether I am to have my reward in the end or not."

His tone was properly beseeching, but stealing a shy look at him, Meg saw that his eyes were merry as well as tender. This nettled her. She felt excited and strange, and not knowing what else to do, followed a capricious impulse, and, withdrawing her hands, said petulantly, "I don't choose. Please go away and let me be!"

Poor Mr. Brooke looked as if his lovely castle in the air was tumbling about his ears, for he had never seen Meg in such a mood before.

"Do you really mean that?" he asked anxiously.

"Yes, I do. I don't want to be worried about such things."

"Mayn't I hope you'll change your mind by-and-by?"

He was grave and pale now. He just stood looking at her so wistfully, so tenderly, that she found her heart relenting in spite of herself.

What would have happened next I cannot say, if Aunt March had not come hobbling in at this interesting minute.

TRACK 15

A FUTURE MARRIAGE

Meg started as if she had seen a ghost, and Mr. Brooke vanished into the study.

"Bless me, what's all this?" cried the old lady with a rap of her cane as she glanced from the pale young gentleman to the scarlet young lady. "There's mischief going on, and I insist upon knowing what it is."

"We were only talking. Mr. Brooke came for his umbrella," began Meg.

"Brooke? That boy's tutor? Ah! I understand now. You haven't gone and accepted him, child?" cried Aunt March. "I've something to say to you. Tell me, do you mean to marry this Rook? If you do, not one penny of my money ever goes to you," said the old lady impressively.

"I shall marry whom I please, Aunt March, and you can leave your money to anyone you like," she said, nodding her head with a resolute air.

Aunt March saw that she had begun wrong, "Now, Meg, my dear, be reasonable and take my advice. You ought to marry well and help your family. This Rook is poor and hasn't got any rich relations, has he?"

"No."

"He hasn't any business, has he?"

"Not yet. Mr. Laurence is going to help him."

"That won't last long. James Laurence is a crotchety old fellow and not to be depended on. I thought you had more sense, Meg."

"I couldn't do better if I waited half my life! John is good and wise; he's willing to work and sure to get on."

"He knows you have got rich relations, child. That's the secret of his liking, I suspect."

"Aunt March, how dare you say such a thing? John is above such meanness, and I won't listen to you a minute if you talk so," cried Meg indignantly, "My John wouldn't marry for money, any more than I would."

"Well, I wash my hands of the whole affair! I'm done with you forever."

And, slamming the door in Meg's face, Aunt March drove off in high dudgeon. Meg stood for a moment, undecided whether to laugh or cry. Before she could make up her mind, she was taken possession of by Mr. Brooke, who said all in one breath, "I couldn't help hearing, Meg. Thank you for defending me, and Aunt March for proving that you do care for me a little bit. And I needn't go away, but may stay and be happy?"

Here was another fine chance to make the crushing speech and the stately exit, but Meg never thought of doing either, and disgraced herself forever in Jo's eyes by meekly whispering, "Yes, John."

Jo came softly downstairs, paused an instant at the parlor door, and hearing no sound within, smiled with a satisfied expression, saying to herself, "She has seen him away as we planned; I'll go and hear the fun, and have a good laugh over it."

But poor Jo never got her laugh, for she was transfixed upon the threshold by a spectacle which held her there. She beheld John Brooke serenely sitting on the sofa, with the strong-minded sister enthroned upon his knee and wearing an expression of the most abject submission. Jo gave a sort of gasp; Meg jumped up, looking both proud and shy, but "that man," as Jo called him, actually laughed and said coolly, as he kissed the astonished newcomer, "Sister Jo, congratulate us!"

Jo vanished without a word. Rushing upstairs, she startled the invalids by exclaiming tragically as she burst into the room, "Oh, do somebody go down quick! John Brooke is acting dreadfully, and Meg likes it!"

Mr. and Mrs. March left the room with speed; Jo cried and scolded tempestuously as she told the awful news to Beth and Amy. The little girls, however, considered it a most agreeable and interesting event, and Jo got little comfort from them, so she went up to her refuge in the garret.

The tea bell rang before he had finished describing to her parents the paradise which he meant to earn for Meg, and he proudly took her in to supper, both looking so happy that Jo hadn't the heart to be jealous or dismal. Laurie came prancing in, overflowing with good spirits, bearing a great bridal-looking bouquet for "Mrs. John Brooke."

"I knew Brooke would have it all his own way, he always does; for when he makes up his mind to accomplish anything, it's done though the sky falls. You don't look festive, ma'am, what's the matter?" asked Laurie, following Jo into a corner of the parlor.

"I don't approve of the match. You can't know how hard it is for me to give up Meg," sighed Jo.

"You've got me, anyhow. I'll stand by you, Jo, all the days of my life. Upon my word I will!"

"I know you will, and I'm ever so much obliged. You are always a great comfort to me, Teddy," returned Jo.

"Don't you wish you could take a look forward and see where we shall all be in three years' time?" asked Laurie.

"I think not, for I might see something sad, and everyone looks so happy now, I don't believe they could be much improved."

And Jo's eyes went slowly round the room, brightening as they looked, for the prospect was a pleasant one.

HEAR IT READ IT

A LITTLE PRINCESS

Frances Hodgson Burnett

Read by Lucy Whybrow

Sara Crewe was born in India and sent to school in England, where she is treated warmly by the school's owner—greedy Miss Minchin—who hopes to gain a piece of the family fortune. But Sara's wealthy father dies, leaving her penniless. Miss Minchin turns Sara into a servant, though Sara finds the strength to survive by using her imagination.

$9.99 U.S/$10.99 CAN/£6.99 UK
ISBN-13: 978-1-4022-1312-0
ISBN-10: 1-4022-1312-3

Hear It · Read It

The Secret Garden

Frances Hodgson Burnett

Read by Jenny Agutter

Mary Lennox doesn't want to move to England to live with her uncle, but she has no choice. At first she hates her uncle's cold house, the gardens, and moors that surround it, and the servants with their funny way of talking. And at night, she hears a child crying, but the servants insist it's only the wind. Curious in spite of herself, Mary wanders the house and gardens and discovers that both are full of secrets.

$9.99 U.S/$10.99 CAN/£6.99 UK

ISBN-13: 978-1-4022-1244-4
ISBN-10: 1-4022-1244-5

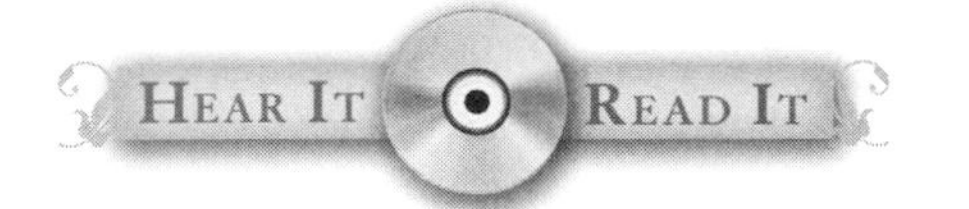

BLACK BEAUTY

THE AUTOBIOGRAPHY OF A HORSE

Anna Sewell

Read by Jonathan Keeble

Black Beauty teaches everyone he meets the true meaning of courage and loyalty. From escaping a burning barn to saving the life of his owner, every day is full of adventure. But he longs for a family to love him for the gentle horse he is. Will he ever find the perfect home?

$9.99 U.S/$10.99 CAN/£6.99 UK

ISBN-13: 9781402211683
ISBN-10: 1402211686

About the Author

Louisa May Alcott was born on November 29, 1832, in Pennsylvania. She spent much of her childhood in Massachusetts with her mother and father and three sisters. Alcott grew up a tomboy, just like her character Jo March. Also like Jo, she began writing at an early age, even writing plays for her sisters to act out. Alcott came from a poor family and worked a variety of jobs to help her family survive. Louisa May Alcott published her first book, *Flower Fables*, in 1854. She is best known for *Little Women* and the sequels that followed it.